i AM LOVABLE™

by Kimberly Dawn

Balboa Press books may be ordered through booksellers or by contacting:

Balboa Press
A Division of Hay House
1663 Liberty Drive
Bloomington, IN 47403
www.balboapress.com
1 (877) 407-4847

ISBN: 978-1-9822-3279-5 (hc)
ISBN: 978-1-9822-3278-8 (e)
Library of Congress Control Number: 2019911605

Printed in China.

Balboa Press rev. date: 09/04/2019

This is Kimberly Dawn. She
feels sad and unlovable –

When she goes to school, the kids tease her, push her, and pull her hair. They call her names and make fun of her because she is different from them.

After school, she goes to visit her aunt to find out if she is lovable. Her aunt is unkind and cruel. She tells Kimberly Dawn, “You just aren’t cool.”

This makes Kimberly Dawn think maybe she isn't lovable.

She thinks if she changes the way she looks on the outside, maybe she will be more lovable.

What could she do to change her appearance? Maybe if she changed her hair, she would fit in.

FASHION

She imagines the way she might look as her new self. She wonders how she could get a different hairstyle. Possibly a new colour and not so many curls might make her lovable.

Before long, she comes up with an idea. She decides she will give herself a new haircut. Maybe then she will become lovable and will fit in.

But when Kimberly Dawn's mother finds out, she gets very angry and punishes Kimberly Dawn.

This makes her feel even more unlovable, lonely, and sad.

She wonders who can help her find out if she is lovable.

She can't talk to the other kids; they will just make fun of her. And the grown-ups don't understand and don't have the patience or time for her.

Feeling sad and even more unlovable, Kimberly Dawn finds a quiet spot in the forest to be alone.

Just as she gets very quiet, she hears a little voice deep down inside herself. ***Kimberly Dawn, you are beautiful, funny, creative, talented, and special.***

"I am?" says Kimberly Dawn.

Of course you are. Think about the talents and abilities you have that are unique and special to you.

Kimberly Dawn sits and quietly listens to her inner voice. She starts imagining all the amazing things she *can* do.

She can draw captivating pictures. She can play exquisite music. And she can write thrilling stories.

The positive thoughts keep coming from deep down inside her self. She's loving, caring, compassionate, and fun.

She asks her little self, “Does that mean I’m lovable?”

Of course you are. All of those qualities are what make you lovable!

At that moment, something magical happens. Kimberly Dawn realizes she does have what it takes to be lovable. She just needs to believe it for herself.

Even if the other kids at school or the adults in her life didn't think so, she knows she must be lovable.

Soon enough, she starts creating works of art, composing beautiful songs, and writing bestselling storybooks.

Then, something amazing happens, the other kids start to see how creative and talented Kimberly Dawn is.

Kids
Wheel Pose
Cobra Pose
Locust Pose
Child's Pose
LOVE
I am strong.
I am kind.
I am brave.
I am friendly.

Before long, they too want to have curly red hair and be creative like her!

This is when Kimberly Dawn realizes that who you really are is on the inside.

It is at this moment that Kimberly Dawn knows and truly believes that she IS lovable.